The Aunt in Our House

by ANGELA JOHNSON • pictures by DAVID SOMAN

ORCHARD BOOKS • NEW YORK

Orchard Books, 95 Madison Avenue, New York, NY 10016

Manufactured in the United States of America. Printed by Barton Press, Inc. Bound by Horowitz/Rae. Book design by Jean Krulis. The text of this book is set in 18 point Korinna. The illustrations are watercolor and pastel reproduced in full color.

10 9 8 7 6 5 4 3 2 1

Library of Congress Cataloging-in-Publication Data. Johnson, Angela. The aunt in our house / by Angela Johnson ; pictures by David Soman.   p.   cm. "A Richard Jackson book"—Half t.p. Summary: When the Aunt comes to live with them, the entire family enjoys her company and helps her forget about the home she has lost. ISBN 0-531-09502-9. — ISBN 0-531-08852-9 (lib. bdg.)   [1. Aunts—Fiction.]   I. Soman, David, ill. II. Title.   PZ7.J629Au   1996   95-30643

*T*he sun shines brighter
through the front window in our house
since The Aunt came.
It makes us warmer in winter.

A willow tree shades the window in summer,
and is very old, and protects us,
The Aunt says.

The Aunt came to stay
on a Sunday when the backyard buzzed with bees
and Sister and me sat in the wildflowers,
waiting for her.

She brought a fish in a bowl
and a chair that she sat under the tree.

She said that we were hers now.
The Aunt was ours too.
So we watched The Aunt in our house.

The Aunt helps Mama
weave rugs and blankets
as they listen to the radio
in the back room.

She keeps the windows open, and sometimes
the yarn blows around the room,
wrapping me and Sister in color.

The Aunt in our house
let Daddy paint her picture.
She sat real still and sometimes winked at us.

When me and Sister
wake up in the morning,
we smile up at the painting
of The Aunt smiling at us.

The Aunt in our house
plays a trumpet
and gives me and Sister lessons.

On rainy days
she helps us find the biggest puddles . . .
and says shoes aren't important.

But sometimes
The Aunt in our house
is quiet
and looks out the window all day.

Mama says she misses her home,
even with the picture painting
and the days that shoes aren't important.

So me and Sister
watch The Aunt in our house, and wait
until the sun starts to shine in her face
and warm us all over.

Then The Aunt sits beside me and Sister
and tells us about the old willow tree
that shades and protects us in our house.